PUFFIN BOOKS

MR MAJEIKA JOINS THE CIRCUS

Humphrey Carpenter (1946–2005), the author and creator of *Mr Majeika*, was born and educated in Oxford. He went to a school called the Dragon School where exciting things often happened and there were some very odd teachers – you could even call it magical! He became a full-time writer in 1975 and was the author of many award-winning biographies. As well as the *Mr Majeika* titles, his children's books also include *Shakespeare Without the Boring Bits* and *More Shakespeare Without the Boring Bits*. He wrote plays for radio and theatre and founded the children's drama group The Mushy Pea Theatre Company. He played the tuba, double bass, bass saxophone and keyboard.

Humphrey once said, 'The nice thing about being a writer is that you can make magic happen without learning tricks. Words are the only tricks you need. I can write: "He floated up to the ceiling, and a baby rabbit came out of his pocket, grew wings, and flew away." And you will believe that it really happened! That's magic, isn't it?'

Books by Humphrey Carpenter

MR MAJEIKA
MR MAJEIKA AND THE DINNER LADY
MR MAJEIKA AND THE GHOST TRAIN
MR MAJEIKA AND THE HAUNTED HOTEL
MR MAJEIKA AND THE LOST SPELL BOOK
MR MAJEIKA AND THE MUSIC TEACHER
MR MAJEIKA AND THE SCHOOL BOOK WEEK
MR MAJEIKA AND THE SCHOOL CARETAKER
MR MAJEIKA AND THE SCHOOL INSPECTOR
MR MAJEIKA AND THE SCHOOL PLAY
MR MAJEIKA AND THE SCHOOL TRIP
MR MAJEIKA JOINS THE CIRCUS
MR MAJEIKA ON THE INTERNET
MR MAJEIKA VANISHES

THE PUFFIN BOOK OF CLASSIC
CHILDREN'S STORIES (Ed.)

SHAKESPEARE WITHOUT THE BORING BITS
MORE SHAKESPEARE WITHOUT THE
BORING BITS

HUMPHREY CARPENTER

Mr Majeika Joins
the Circus

Illustrated by Frank Rodgers

PUFFIN

PUFFIN BOOKS

Published by the Penguin Group
Penguin Books Ltd, 80 Strand, London WC2R 0RL, England
Penguin Group (USA) Inc., 375 Hudson Street, New York, New York 10014, USA
Penguin Group (Canada), 90 Eglinton Avenue East, Suite 700, Toronto, Ontario, Canada M4P 2Y3
(a division of Pearson Penguin Canada Inc.)
Penguin Ireland, 25 St Stephen's Green, Dublin 2, Ireland (a division of Penguin Books Ltd)
Penguin Group (Australia), 250 Camberwell Road, Camberwell, Victoria 3124, Australia
(a division of Pearson Australia Group Pty Ltd)
Penguin Books India Pvt Ltd, 11 Community Centre, Panchsheel Park, New Delhi – 110 017, India
Penguin Group (NZ), 67 Apollo Drive, Rosedale, North Shore 0632, New Zealand
(a division of Pearson New Zealand Ltd)
Penguin Books (South Africa) (Pty) Ltd, 24 Sturdee Avenue, Rosebank, Johannesburg 2196, South Africa

Penguin Books Ltd, Registered Offices: 80 Strand, London WC2R 0RL, England

puffinbooks.com

First published 2006
This edition published 2010 for The Book People Ltd,
Hall Wood Avenue, Haydock, St Helens WA11 9UL
001 – 10 9 8 7 6 5 4 3 2 1

Text copyright © Mari Prichard, 2006
Illustrations copyright © Frank Rodgers, 2006
All rights reserved

The moral right of the author and illustrator has been asserted

Set in Palatino

Printed in Great Britain by Clays Ltd, St Ives plc

British Library Cataloguing in Publication Data
A CIP catalogue record for this book is available from the British Library

ISBN: 978-0-141-33697-8

www.greenpenguin.co.uk

Penguin Books is committed to a sustainable future
for our business, our readers and our planet.
The book in your hands is made from paper
certified by the Forest Stewardship Council.

With thanks to Gifford's Circus for inspiring this book with brilliant acts which are NOT old or tired . . .

To Ben, Ollie and Freddie for suggesting lots of it . . .

And to Caitlin and Anna for making it even better.

Contents

1. *Billy's Not So Bold*

Billy Balance was frightened.

He knew there wasn't a sensible
reason to be frightened. But he couldn't
help it. His knees kept wobbling. And
if they wobbled when he began to
cross the rope, that would be it. He
would fall.

Billy Balance was a slack-rope walker.
You probably don't know what a slack-
rope walker is. Maybe you think I'm
making a mistake and really mean a
tightrope walker. Well, a slack-rope
walker is like a tightrope walker. Up to a
point. Both of them walk across a rope,

which is stretched from one side of a
circus tent to the other. Except a
tightrope is tight and firm to stand on,
and a slack rope isn't. It just hangs
loosely across the tent, in a gentle curve,
and you can't imagine that anyone could
ever walk across it.

In fact there are very few people in the
world who can. And one of them was
Billy Balance. He didn't just walk across
it. He *danced*. When he reached the
middle of the rope he would produce a

violin from inside his coat. He would begin to play an Irish jig, a bouncy tune that soon had the audience clapping. He jumped up and down in time to the music. He waved his left leg, and then his right leg, so far in the air that you could see it was almost impossible to do that without falling off the rope. And he finished his act by jumping high, and then spinning round in mid-air.

Nobody else in the entire world has ever done that. And the audience went wild.

If you asked Billy how he did it, he wouldn't be able to tell you. It was something he'd been taught when he was a tiny child. Maybe his teacher could do magic. Or maybe he was just very good at balancing. But whatever the explanation, Billy now had a different secret. He was losing his nerve.

Last night he had nearly fallen off the rope. Not just at the end of his act when he was jumping and spinning, but from the very beginning of his act he had felt his feet slipping. It was as if the air itself was trying to pull him down. And that was very frightening, because the air had always been his friend.

Perhaps it was because he was getting older, and had begun to wonder himself how he did his act. That was a mistake, like when you're riding a bike. If you start to wonder why you're not falling off, then falling off is probably what you will do.

The bell rang, which marked the end of the interval. Outside the tent, the audience hurried to finish their ice creams and drinks and candy floss and hot dogs and crisps, and started to make their way back to their seats. The ringmaster, wearing his top hat, long red coat and riding trousers, went to get the audience to hurry up. In five minutes the music would begin, and that would be the sign for Billy to run into the circus ring and start making rude noises at the band.

But Billy didn't want to go out there again. He was more frightened than ever and he was sure he was going to fall. The actual fall probably wouldn't hurt him too much – it wasn't very far – but the shame would be terrible, and it would be the end of his work in the circus.

Maybe he should run away. He opened a flap in the canvas, and peered out. If he was quick, he could make a dash for it. But no – there was a school party, dawdling on their way back to the tent. One of the boys was having an argument with the teacher. 'Hamish,' the teacher was saying, 'I have had enough

of you. And you know what happens
when I get cross.'

'Yah boo sucks,' answered the boy
cheekily. 'You wouldn't dare do magic
here, Mr Majeika.'

They passed Billy and went to their
seats. The band started to play.

And for Billy, it was time to begin.

2. *The Strongest Bigmore in the World*

Hamish Bigmore hadn't wanted to go to the circus. 'What's the point of looking at a load of silly clowns who aren't funny?' he sneered. 'And a lot of mangy old lions and tigers who wouldn't hurt a flea?'

Jody shook her head. 'There won't be any lions and tigers,' she said. 'Most circuses don't have them any more. They don't want people to say they're cruel to animals. They have acrobats instead.'

'That's feeble,' mocked Hamish Bigmore, who was the worst-behaved boy in Class Three. 'Who wants to see stupid old acrobats?'

'We do,' said Thomas, who was one of the twins.

'You bet we do,' said Pete, who was the other one. 'Look, Mr Majeika, we can do some real acrobat stunts!' Pete bent over, and Thomas jumped up and stood on his back. At least, he tried to. But he was going too fast, and he shot over Pete's back and crashed straight into Mr

Potter, the head teacher, who was coming into the classroom.

'I was just bringing your tickets for Tottle's Circus, Mr Majeika,' said Mr Potter, when he had picked himself up off the floor. 'They're absolutely free,' he went on. 'Mr Tottle, who runs the circus, has had trouble getting people to go to it this week, so he's giving away tickets to schoolchildren, in the hope that they will tell their friends how good the circus is, and then people will start going to it. I hope you enjoy the trip, everyone.' And off he went.

'Please will somebody explain to me exactly what a circus is?' asked Mr Majeika, who had been a wizard before he became a teacher, and often didn't understand things about the ordinary world.

'Well,' said Jody, 'it's people doing clever and difficult things, like riding a

horse but standing up on its back, or
flying through the air from one trapeze to
another. Do you get the idea, Mr Majeika?'

'I suppose so,' said Mr Majeika
doubtfully. 'But if these things are so
difficult to do, why don't people use
magic?'

'You remember, Mr Majeika!' said
Jody. 'We don't use magic in this world.
And *you're* not supposed to do any now
that you're a teacher and no longer a
wizard.'

'Oh yes. Silly me,' he said.

'Oh, Mr Majeika, it doesn't matter, we don't mind you doing magic at all,' said Thomas.

'We certainly don't,' said Pete. And they all set off for the circus – even Hamish Bigmore, though he was still grumbling a bit.

It's not surprising that Tottle's Circus wasn't selling lots of tickets. For years it had spent each summer touring round the whole country, and Mr Tottle was tired, and so were many of his performers.

But when Class Three arrived at the field near St Barty's School where the circus had pitched its tent, they were all very excited. Jody hurried off to look at the horses in their stable, and Thomas and Pete wanted to hear all about the acrobats and the clowns from the girl who was selling programmes. 'The chief clown is called Scratchy,' she told them.

'He does a very funny act with an old suitcase and some silly hats.'

But when the band began to play, and the performance started, it was all a bit disappointing. The first act was a tired old elephant, who wandered round the ring once or twice, before leaving the tent and going to sleep next to the caravans. After this came a dancing horse, except that it didn't really dance; it just shuffled around the ring, hardly lifting up its hoofs. The woman who was looking after it was dressed in a faded costume, and she looked worn out

and unwell. Jody, who had been looking forward to seeing beautiful horses dancing elegantly, was very disappointed – she could see that the horse looked as unhappy as the woman.

Then came Scratchy the Clown. He tried to do funny things with his suitcase, and the various hats he pulled out of it, but none of Class Three laughed. 'I could do better than that,' Pete muttered to Hamish Bigmore.

'So could I,' said Hamish, and when Scratchy took his bow, Hamish actually booed.

'Hamish!' said Jody, very shocked. 'How can you be so horrible to him?'

Hamish gave a nasty laugh. 'He's hopeless. And I reckon the next act will be even worse.' He pointed at his programme. 'It's a strong man.'

Mr Tottle cracked his whip and announced through the microphone: 'My lords, ladies and gentlemen, boys and girls, Tottle's Circus is proud to present, all the way from Russia, Ivan the Terrible!'

The band played some sinister Russian-style music, a curtain sprang open, and into the ring stepped the strongest-looking man Class Three had ever seen. He had arms as thick as tree trunks, and his whole body looked as if he were made of massive muscles. He bowed to the audience, swung his arms for a moment, and then bent down and slowly picked up an iron bar with enormous weights at each end.

The audience clapped – all except Hamish Bigmore. 'He's a fake,' Hamish muttered to Jody and, before she could stop him, Hamish had got up from his seat and walked into the circus ring. 'My lords, ladies and gentlemen, boys and girls,' he said into the microphone, copying Mr Tottle, 'you may think you've been watching the strongest man in the world, but now you're going to see the strongest Bigmore in the world! Look!' And he bent down and picked up the huge iron bar with just one hand.

It wasn't iron at all. Ivan the Terrible was beginning to get old and tired, like so many of the performers in Tottle's Circus, and the bar was made of something much lighter than iron – wood and plastic. It weighed next to nothing.

When he saw that Hamish had guessed his secret, Ivan gave a terrible roar and began to chase Hamish round

the circus ring. The trouble was, Ivan got
out of breath very quickly. He stopped
for a moment – and Hamish grabbed the
fake iron bar, and used it to wallop Ivan
on the bottom.

Ivan roared again and chased Hamish
out of the tent and away into the
distance.

The rest of Class Three were delighted
with the unexpected finale to the
otherwise dull first half. But then, after
the interval, came Billy Balance.

16

3. Billy's Going to Fall

It was Billy's job to open the second half
of the show. He came on looking very
smart, in a top hat, a white tie, and a
black tailcoat and trousers. The band was
playing, and he made a few jokes about
the musicians, pretending to annoy them.
This made them put down their
instruments and chase him round the
circus ring.

There was a ladder that led to a
wooden perch at one end of the slack
rope, and Billy ran up it to get away
from the musicians. One of them started
to climb after him. At this point Billy

was supposed to go out on to the rope to escape. The musician would stop chasing and stare as Billy stepped on the rope. Billy would then pretend to be frightened, go wobbly, and look as if he were just about to fall off. But then he would suddenly save himself and make it look easy and funny and magical.

Billy began his act in the usual way, but he was shaking like a leaf all the time, and anyone who knew him could see that he wasn't *pretending* to be wobbly. It was real, and it would be a matter of seconds before he fell off.

If he fell off, the shame and embarrassment would be terrible. However bad things got at Tottle's, no one had ever given up their act halfway through. The circus rule was never to stop, and never to let the smile slip from your face for even a moment.

The rope swayed from side to side, and Billy tried to do what had always been second nature to him – just lean the right way, very quickly, to stay balanced. But his feet were all over the place, and his arms were waving wildly, as if he were trying to find things to hold on to.

He hadn't taken out his violin; it would be more than enough if he could just walk across the rope without disaster. He waved his hat. He tried to keep smiling, then . . .

Whoops! There he went at last – he'd

finally missed his footing and was falling.

Oh no, he wasn't! He had started to fall, but some sort of giant invisible hand seemed to scoop him up and put him back on the slack rope.

And then it picked him up again, bouncing him along the rope as if he were a puppet and making him dance and jump and spin; it even made him give a bow to the audience when he reached the far end.

Everyone went wild. Even people who had been to circuses lots and lots of times had never seen anything like it in their lives.

'Hooray!' shouted Thomas and Pete, at the tops of their voices, as Billy Balance took a bow, looking as surprised as everyone else.

Only Jody was silent. She looked at Mr Majeika. He was clapping, but he looked

rather tired, as if he had been doing a difficult spell.

'Mr Majeika,' Jody said, 'were you doing some magic just then?'

Mr Majeika smiled. 'Let's just say I gave him a little help,' he said. And he put his finger on his lips, meaning that she shouldn't say anything about it to anyone.

4. *St Barty's School Circus*

When Mr Majeika took Class Three back
to school they were all very happy and
talking about Billy's amazing
performance.

So was Mr Tottle. The next morning he
called Billy Balance into the ringmaster's
caravan, and patted him on the back.
'Well done, lad,' he said. 'One moment I
thought you were going to take a
tumble. Next thing, you were zooming
around like a space-rocket. How did you
do it, then? No, I won't ask you that –
I've learnt never to ask circus folk how
they do their acts. It's your secret. But

make sure you do it at every performance. Don't forget! I'll be watching.'

Poor Billy! He had gone, as they say, from the frying pan into the fire. He knew very well that his amazing flying performance had been made to happen by somebody else, probably somebody in the audience. And he thought he might know who.

He remembered one of the schoolchildren talking to a man with glasses and a beard about magic. And Billy had been in the circus long enough to recognize a magician when he saw one! If only they could meet, then maybe Billy could find out what was going on.

Then Billy had a stroke of luck. He went for a walk, to help him think things over. And, sure enough, who should he see but the man who had been sitting with the children.

'Hello, Mr Magician!' said Billy.

Class Three were all ready for morning school, but there was no sign of Mr Majeika, so they turned the classroom into a circus.

'My lords, ladies and gentlemen, girls and boys,' called out Thomas, who had decided to be the ringmaster, 'St Barty's School Circus is proud to present the

24

most elegant equestrian act in the United Kingdom – please put your hands together to welcome . . . Miss Jody!'

'What's an "equestrian act"?' asked Pete.

'It means an act with horses,' said Jody.

'But we don't have any horses,' said Pete.

'Yes we do,' said Jody. 'Get down on your knees!'

Pete grumbled, but in the end he agreed to be the horse. He trotted round the classroom with Jody on his back. 'Dance a bit more!' said Jody, and Pete tried to. But Jody was so heavy that he soon fell in a heap and tipped her on to the floor.

'Never mind the little accident there, my lords, ladies and gentlemen, boys and girls,' said Thomas in his ringmaster voice. 'It's time to bring on the clowns.

So please put your hands together and give a big warm welcome to the chief clown at St Barty's Circus – yes, here he is, it's Smelly!'

'It's *who*?' asked Pete, amazed. 'You can't have a clown called Smelly!'

'Why not?' asked Thomas. 'The clown at Tottle's Circus is called Scratchy. What's the difference?'

'Anyway,' said Pete, 'who's going to be this clown?'

'I am,' said Thomas.

'But you're the ringmaster,' objected
Pete. 'You can't be the clown as well.'

'Why not? I'm in charge of this circus.'

'No you're not.'

'Yes I am.' And they had a fight, with
Pete calling Thomas 'smelly', and
Thomas being just as rude in return.
Then suddenly the classroom door
opened, and in jumped a lion.

Afterwards, Jody said that she had known all along that the lion was really Hamish Bigmore. In that case, Thomas had asked, why had she screamed her head off, and jumped up on the table, knocking over piles of books and nearly sending the classroom fish tank crashing to the floor?

In fact they were all terrified at first, and it wasn't until they began to realize that the lion was roaring in rather a squeaky voice that somebody called out, 'It's all right, it's only Hamish Bigmore in a silly old lion costume.' Hamish was roaring and jumping round the classroom, knocking everything over and creating a terrible mess.

The door opened and in came Mr Potter.

All at once, the circus screeched to a halt. 'My lords, ladies and gentlemen, boys and girls,' shouted Thomas in his ringmaster's voice, 'that's the end of this performance by the St Barty's School Circus, and I'm sorry about the mess, Mr Potter, I really am, and we'll clear it all up right away.'

'You certainly will,' said Mr Potter. 'Remind me of your name, boy.'

'Smelly,' said Thomas, and everyone collapsed in helpless laughter.

'Don't be cheeky,' said Mr Potter. 'You're all going to have to do detention. And where on earth has Mr Majeika got to? It's not like him to be as late as this.'

5. *Mr Majeika Says No*

Mr Majeika was walking hurriedly to school. He usually walked, although if it was a very sunny day he sometimes flew. He had first arrived at St Barty's School on a magic carpet. But, as a very experienced wizard, he didn't need a carpet to fly on. It was just a more comfortable way of travelling long distances.

When he flew to school, he was usually careful to make himself invisible, just in case he ran into – or flew into – anyone who might recognize him. Often, he flew invisibly along a crowded shopping street. But, of course, no one could see him, so they had no idea that one of their children's teachers was zooming along the street, just above their heads.

Once or twice, Mr Majeika had forgotten to make himself invisible, and he had flown into Mr Potter. But the head teacher never seemed to notice if Mr Majeika did magic things. When Mr Majeika flew into him, Mr Potter just said: 'Now, Majeika, you really must look where you're going.'

I should perhaps explain to you that, although Mr Majeika wasn't supposed to do any magic now that he had become a teacher, the same rule didn't apply when he was at home and entirely by himself. When he knew no one could see him, he could certainly do magic without getting into trouble. And, in fact, he very often did.

For example, Mr Majeika's alarm clock

was actually a magic clock, and it woke
him up every morning by releasing a
huge black crow, which flew up and
down his bedroom, cawing loudly until
he got out of bed.

Mr Majeika cleaned his teeth with a
magic toothbrush. Or rather, the
toothbrush did the cleaning for him.
When it saw him coming, it would jump
up and down on the edge of the
washbasin, and shout in a squeaky voice:

'Don't forget your teeth! Don't forget your teeth!' Then, it would squeeze the toothpaste from the tube and on to its bristles. All that Mr Majeika had to do was open his mouth. The brush did all the hard work.

His clothes dressed him, his shoes tied neat little bows with their laces, and his front-door key turned itself in the lock, so that burglars couldn't get in. Then his hat and coat – *not* his pointed wizard's hat – put themselves on him, and off he walked, or flew, to school.

He was very careful that nobody ever saw these strange goings-on.

But this morning, Mr Majeika wasn't flying to school, and when Billy Balance came looking for him, he saw Mr Majeika walking through the streets like any ordinary person.

'Hello, Mr Magician!' Billy called, and

at first Mr Majeika paid no attention. Ever since the circus performance, he had been worried that Billy Balance would come looking for him like this, to ask about the magic that Mr Majeika had used to rescue him. Mr Majeika didn't want to admit to Billy that there had been some magic. He was certainly disobeying orders by doing magic in such a public place as the circus, with hundreds of people sitting in the audience and watching. But he had felt sorry for Billy.

'Hello, Mr Magician!' called Billy again.

'Hello, Billy,' said Mr Majeika. 'But, sshh!' he warned. 'I'm not supposed to do anything magical. I'm glad that I was able to help you, but please don't expect me to do it again. And now I really must go to teach my class at school.'

Billy looked miserable. 'But you saved

my life,' he said. 'Or at least you saved me from losing my job at the circus, which is almost the same thing.'

'Does the circus mean that much to you?' Mr Majeika asked.

'You bet it does,' said Billy Balance. 'It's the most exciting place in the whole world.'

'It must be very hard work,' said Mr Majeika.

Billy nodded. 'Yes, it is,' he said, 'but it's also like being on holiday all year! I'll try to explain.

'Every year,' Billy went on, 'you're on the road, travelling from one end of the country to the other. Not just driving in a boring old motor car, oh no! You're riding in a lovely old-fashioned, hand-painted showman's caravan, pulled by a magnificent horse.

'Sometimes you come to a new town or village at night, and when the morning sun comes up, you see this new place for the first time.

'After that, everybody joins in the enormous job of putting up the tent – the Big Top. We lay it out on the grass, and Mr Tottle calls out orders. Slowly, very slowly, but steadily, the Big Top rises from the ground, like a big striped castle, with flags of all colours flying on the top of it.

'The circus has come to town! We march through the streets, playing musical instruments, to make sure that

everyone who lives there knows that we've arrived.

'And then it's time for the show to begin! When the music starts, you feel a thrill that's like nothing on earth – a funny mixture of nerves and excitement, and you can hardly wait till your own act begins. Suddenly you're out there, a great roar comes out from the audience, and you feel happier and more proud than you ever felt in your life.

'After a day or two, it's time to move on again. Part of you is sad to be leaving a place where you've been happy, and the people are friendly, but another part of you is excited at moving on and seeing somewhere new.

'It's a wonderful life, the circus!'

'It sounds it,' said Mr Majeika, sighing a little.

'So why don't you come and join us, Mr Magician?' asked Billy.

'Join you?'

'Yes,' said Billy. 'I need your help, to
make my act work. You helped me by
doing something magical. I need that
help every time I get up on the rope. If
you joined the circus, you could give me
your magical help every day. And of
course you could do your own act as
well.'

'My own act?' asked Mr Majeika.

'Yes,' said Billy. 'A magical conjuring
act. You could make people in the
audience disappear. Whatever you liked.

Haven't you ever wanted to join a circus?'

'I'd never thought of it till now,' said Mr Majeika. 'But I can't. I need to look after the children in my class.'

'They can find another teacher,' said Billy Balance. '*Everyone* wants to run away and join the circus.'

Mr Majeika sighed again. 'I'm sorry, but no,' he said.

Billy Balance looked as if he were going to cry. 'How am I to do my act if you won't help me?' he asked.

'I'm sorry,' said Mr Majeika again, 'but I'm already very late for school. I'm sure if you practised hard, you could get really good at your act again. And now I must say goodbye.'

Billy Balance watched him go. Then he sat down gloomily on a bench, with his head in his hands.

'Having a spot of trouble, are we?'

said a nasty-sounding voice. Billy
looked up.

'What are you doing here, Rubber
Face?' he asked.

Rubber Face was a very strange person
indeed. As his name suggested, his face
seemed to be made of rubber, and he
could make himself look exactly like
anyone that he chose – from the Queen
to a famous pop singer or film star.

Rubber Face often turned up at the

40

circus, and did an act in which he kept changing his appearance. But for much of the time he wasn't there. He would come and go without warning. The circus people found him very creepy.

'Never you mind what I'm doing here,' said Rubber Face. 'I see you have made friends with a certain wizard. Is he going to join the circus?'

'No he isn't,' said Billy Balance. 'He wants to stay as a teacher.'

'We'll see about that,' said Rubber Face. And, as he spoke, his face began to change, until he looked exactly like Jody. 'We'll see about that,' he repeated, and set off down the road, to catch up with Mr Majeika.

6. *Two Jodys?*

Jody had run away to join the circus.

Of course, sensible people like Jody don't run away without telling anyone. But as soon as Mr Potter told Class Three that they would all be given detention, she slipped out of the room before he noticed. The circus was very near her home, so she decided to spend the morning there, and then go home before anyone had realized that she was missing from school.

At least, that was what she was telling herself. In fact she hoped that the circus people would invite her to join them.

Maybe she could look after the horses, or even take part in one of the equestrian acts. She knew that she would have to practise for a very long time to learn all the circus skills, but she was ready for some hard work.

If she succeeded she would be dressed in a lovely spangled jacket, and a glittering top hat, and she would stand on one leg on the horse's back, and

canter round the ring while the band played thrilling music. And then, when the performance was over, she would help to pack up the Big Top, and travel on with the circus to its next town or village. She couldn't wait!

She was walking down the street on her way to the circus when suddenly she saw Mr Majeika coming towards her. Her first idea was to turn round and walk quickly in the opposite direction, in the hope that he wouldn't see her. Then she thought that this would be dishonest. And she had just made up her mind to tell Mr Majeika what had happened – that Mr Potter had given Class Three detention, and she had decided to go off and join the circus – when something very strange happened.

She saw *herself* walking up to Mr Majeika, and saying hello to him.

Jody could see at once that it was

herself. Or rather, she could see that it was somebody who looked exactly like her. The clothes weren't hers, but the face of this new Jody was exactly the face that the real Jody saw in the mirror every morning when she brushed her hair.

She was furious! Who dared to go around pretending to be her? On the other hand it was very clever. She decided to hide in a shop doorway so that she could hear what they were saying.

'Hello, Jody,' said Mr Majeika. 'What are you doing out of school?'

'I'm sorry, Mr Majeika,' said the Pretend Jody – and the voice was exactly like her own. 'You see, we had a message sent to school saying that Billy Balance has had an accident at the circus, and they need your magic powers to make him better. I've been sent to find

you and to tell you to come to the circus
right away.'

'But I was talking to Billy just a
moment ago,' said Mr Majeika, looking
very puzzled. 'He seemed fine, and
he didn't say anything about an
accident.'

'Well, that's what I was told,' said the
Pretend Jody. 'And I think you really
ought to go to the circus and see for
yourself.'

46

'All right,' said Mr Majeika. 'But who is going to look after Class Three?'

'We'll be all right,' said the Pretend Jody. 'Mr Potter has told us that we should practise our circus acts in PE. We are all going to try and have a go on the trapeze.'

Mr Majeika thought for a moment. 'I don't feel very happy about you doing that,' he said. '*You* might have an accident too.'

'Oh no, we won't,' said the Pretend Jody. 'We'll be very careful.'

Mr Majeika thought again. 'All right,' he said. 'But I'll give you a spell to help you when you practise, and promise me you won't get up on to the trapeze until you are sure it's working. It's a simple flying rhyme – you just say:

Those magnificent folk on the flying trapeze,
They fly through the air with the greatest of ease.

Never ask how, and never ask why,

But believe in yourself – you'll be able to fly.

'That should work very well,' said Mr Majeika. 'Go back and try it with everyone else. And I must hurry off to the circus to see what's the matter with poor Billy.'

The real Jody waited while he walked off in the direction of the circus – and the Pretend Jody simply vanished!

Jody thought about following Mr Majeika to see that he wasn't being led into a trap, but she decided that he could always use his magic if he got into a sticky situation. And the thought of using Mr Majeika's spell to practise her own circus act was far too exciting!

So she ran back to the school and went into the classroom. The first person she saw there was Thomas.

'We thought you had run away,' said
Thomas.

'I did mean to,' said Jody. 'But I've
come back because I saw Mr Majeika,
and someone is pretending to be me. It's
all very odd. But I also know that Mr
Majeika has sent us a spell to help us do
circus acts. It might make us just like
Billy Balance. Shall we try it?'

'Of course,' said Pete. 'We'll try it right
away.'

And all of Class Three stood in a circle, holding hands. Jody chanted the spell, and then the others chanted it too:

'Those magnificent folk on the flying trapeze,
  They fly through the air with the greatest of ease.
Never ask how, and never ask why,
  But believe in yourself – you'll be able to fly.'

'Now,' said Jody, 'let's see if it works.'

7. Circus Magic

Mr Majeika had been tricked.

He sat unhappily in Billy Balance's caravan, staring gloomily out of the window. He wanted to get back to school, to see how Class Three were getting on with the spell. He was worried about leaving them with only Mr Potter in charge. But he couldn't escape. He got up and rattled the door handle. The door was locked. He tried the window. It wouldn't open. He was a prisoner.

When he had got to the circus, Billy – of course – was perfectly all right. Nobody could explain why Mr Majeika had been given that message, but as he was now here, Billy persuaded Mr Majeika to sit in one of the seats in the empty Big Top, and try out his magic.

Billy climbed up the ladder to the slack rope, and stepped gingerly on to it. 'Now!' he called to Mr Majeika. 'Do your magic now!'

Mr Majeika tried. He tried very, very hard. But no magic would come.

'It's not working!' shouted Billy. 'Try harder!'

Mr Majeika tried as hard as he could. He muttered the words of the spell that had saved Billy at the circus performance, but all his magic powers had somehow disappeared. The spell wouldn't work. Billy wobbled and fell.

Billy grabbed the slack rope as he fell past it, and held on tight, dangling by his arms. Then he managed to get himself to the ladder, and come down safely.

'Not such a pretty sight, Billy Boy,'
said a voice from the doorway that led
from the Big Top to the backstage area.
Mr Tottle had been watching Billy's
disaster. 'Is this your magician friend?'
he asked, taking a good look at Mr
Majeika. 'Well, I don't think much of his
so-called magic powers.'

'I'm sorry, Mr Tottle,' said Billy. 'I'm
sure he'll get it right at this afternoon's
performance.'

'There isn't going to be a show this afternoon,' said Mr Tottle gloomily. 'We haven't sold enough tickets. They don't seem to like us in this town.'

'That's a pity,' said Billy. 'I like it here, and Mr Majeika lives here, so that's handy if he can help me.'

'No, Billy,' said Mr Tottle, 'we've got to move on. We've got to go to London.'

'London?' Billy was astonished. 'Why on earth do you want to go there, Mr Tottle?'

'Television,' said Mr Tottle. 'I'm friends with a television producer, and he wants to make a programme about my circus. I can't afford to miss that chance. Going on television will make us famous. So we'll go to London and put up the Big Top next door to the studios. And I think Mr Majeika had better come with us. If his magic starts to work again, that could make all the difference for us. Come over here for a moment, Billy.'

Billy went over, and Mr Tottle whispered in his ear: 'Lock him in your caravan!'

Billy frowned. 'I don't like that idea, Mr Tottle,' he said. 'It's not fair on him.'

Now it was Mr Tottle's turn to frown. 'You'll do as you're told, Billy Balance,' he said angrily. 'I don't pay you a wage each week just so that you can fall off that rope. Now get on with it.'

Billy thought for a moment, then asked Mr Majeika to come and have a cup of tea with him in his caravan. Mr Majeika agreed reluctantly, but he said he must get back to school very soon. And as soon as Mr Majeika got inside, Billy had slammed the caravan door shut.

Now Mr Majeika was sitting miserably in the caravan, wondering why none of his magic would work. There was only one person he knew who could block his spells, and he hadn't seen that mischievous witch, Wilhelmina Worlock, for a very long time. As he sat and wondered he suddenly felt a terrible jolt, and one end of the caravan rose up a little. Billy's caravan was being hitched on to the line of wagons, and they were moving.

As Rubber Face watched the last caravan leave he looked very pleased with himself. His face started to change

again, and there stood Wilhelmina
Worlock! She set off for the school.

Class Three were pretty miserable too.
Mr Majeika's rhyme wasn't doing what
they expected. They tried climbing on
the tables and jumping off, but nobody
was able to fly.

'Oh dear,' said Jody, 'perhaps I
remembered it wrong. But I'm sure I
didn't. Why, oh why doesn't it work?'

Just then, Mr Potter came in, sighing.
'There's still no sign of Mr Majeika, so
I'll have to take his class myself. You
may as well have your detention now, I
suppose. I want you all to write these
words out fifty times: "I have never
wanted to run away and join the
circus."' Mr Potter scratched the back of
his neck. 'How odd,' he said. 'Those
aren't the words I meant to say at all.
But they will do. Off you go!'

Class Three all began writing. Jody looked up and, to her surprise, she thought she saw Mr Potter staring into the classroom from outside the window. She looked back at the blackboard and there was Mr Potter again. She put up her hand. 'Mr Potter,' she said.

'Quiet, Jody!' said Mr Potter. 'Or you will have to do fifty more lines.'

'But, Mr Potter,' Jody cried, 'look!' and she pointed to the window.

Mr Potter looked at the window, and saw himself looking back. 'I didn't think we had a mirror there,' he said in his usual vague manner.

As Mr Potter was staring at what he thought was his own reflection, something very strange happened. The classroom melted away, and they all found themselves inside a gigantic circus tent. Everyone in Class Three was wearing circus clothes and the band was playing.

Thomas and Pete were dressed like acrobats, and they were flying around the room. Although they had wanted to be acrobats only that morning, they did not look as if they were enjoying themselves at all. As the music played, they whizzed around the ring, swinging wildly to and fro on trapezes, passing each other in mid-air.

'I feel sick,' yelled Pete.

'Me too,' cried Thomas 'I want to get down!'

Jody was performing the equestrian act of her dreams. But she was beginning to wonder if this was her perfect dream after all. She was standing on one leg on the back of a horse, spinning round and round as the horse galloped in circles round the tent. The horse was going much faster than she had expected, and all this spinning was making her dizzy.

Mr Potter was dressed like a clown,

with a white face and a red nose, and
there was a huge audience pointing and
laughing at him. Every time he tried to
run away his trousers fell down and the
audience laughed even louder.

He was muttering under his breath,
'Just a dream, old chap, just a dream.'
Although he had to admit this was quite
unlike any dream he had ever had
before.

And then in came the lions. Hamish

was dressed as a lion tamer, but he didn't know how to tame lions and they were running wild in the Big Top, roaring at the children, making Melanie burst into tears. But it didn't take much to make Melanie cry.

'Don't panic, children, it's just a dream!' shouted Mr Potter over the noise of the lions. 'I'm sure we'll all wake up in just a moment.'

8. *Fly on the Wall*

This is where you need to know about Mr Tottle's friend who was a television producer.

He wasn't really Mr Tottle's friend at all. He was using Mr Tottle in a nasty way.

His name was Midge. This was a very suitable name for him, because a midge is a very small fly, which you can hardly see, but which gives you a nasty bite. This is what Midge did when he made television programmes about people.

He would say to somebody: 'I'd like to make a programme about you.' Most people got very excited when he said that, because almost everybody wants to be on television. But having a programme made about you by Midge wasn't nice.

He would use hidden cameras, and he would film people so that they looked like stupid idiots. He called these 'fly-on-the-wall' programmes, because a fly can watch people making fools of themselves without being noticed itself. People who had fly-on-the-wall programmes made about them by Midge usually spent the rest of their lives hiding from their friends, and hoping that the programme would be forgotten (which it wasn't).

Midge had planned to make a fly-on-the-wall programme about Tottle's Circus. He'd had a tip-off from someone called Rubber Face that it was in a bad way – that Ivan the Terrible was using fake weights, and that Billy Balance was losing his nerve. Midge thought it would be funny to make a programme about a circus that was collapsing. He rather hoped there would be an accident during a performance, and that he might manage to film it. He didn't care if people got hurt, so long as he got a good programme out of it.

This is why he had asked Mr Tottle to come and see him when he was next in London. He hadn't expected Mr Tottle to turn up at the television studio without warning, and he certainly hadn't expected Mr Tottle to bring the entire circus with him.

Midge was standing in his office, on the eleventh floor of the television company building, drinking a cup of coffee, when he saw a strange procession coming up the road.

A row of caravans was being pulled by an enormous elephant, and after the caravans came a couple of very old

lorries, piled very high with canvas. A big
sign hanging round the elephant's neck
said 'TOTTLE'S CIRCUS ON TOUR'.

The elephant was called Hannibal,
and he was very old. Although Mr
Tottle let him wander around the ring
for a few minutes at the start of each
performance, he mostly spent his time
resting, so that he would have the

energy to pull the caravans when the circus left town. This time he had to pull the lorries as well, because they had broken down.

'Look at that rubbishy old circus,' said Midge, laughing nastily as Hannibal the elephant stopped at the main gate of the television building. 'I wonder what it's doing here.' He had forgotten about his invitation to Mr Tottle.

Midge's telephone rang. He picked it up. It was the security man at the main gate. 'I've got a circus here that's asking for you,' he said to Midge. 'Chap in charge is an old fellow called Tottle. Says you invited him here.'

Midge spilt his coffee all down his shirt front. 'I didn't mean the entire circus to come here,' he spluttered. 'Kick them all out!'

At the main gate, the security man put

down the phone. 'I'm to kick you all
out,' he told Mr Tottle.

'Just you try!' said Mr Tottle.

So the security man tried, which was a
mistake. He kicked Hannibal the
elephant, and Hannibal got a bit cross
about this. He picked up the security
man with his trunk and threw him into
the ornamental pond near the gates of
the television building. Then he ripped
the barrier gate out of its socket, and
lumbered into the car park, pulling the
entire circus behind him.

'Well, we've arrived,' said Mr Tottle.
'Let's get ready to perform on television.'

Mr Majeika was fed up. He had been
stuck in the caravan all the way to
London, and every time it turned a
corner, the cups and saucers on the table
fell on to the floor. Mr Majeika had to
hold on to stop himself falling off his

seat. The journey had taken a very long time, so he was relieved when they finally stopped. When it was safe to stand up, he looked out of the window to see what was going on.

He could see the circus people setting up the Big Top in what looked like a car park. Hannibal the elephant was lifting up all the poles, and the acrobats were climbing up them to hang the canvas over the top. In the blink of an eye the big tent was up. Mr Majeika couldn't help feeling impressed. He'd never seen anybody work so quickly without the use of magic.

Just as he was thinking this, the door of the caravan burst open and in rushed Billy Balance. 'Oh, Mr Majeika,' he panted, 'you must come and do your spell for me again. The circus is going to be on television in just a few minutes, and I'm terrified that the whole world is going to watch me fall.'

Doing a spell for Billy was the last
thing that Mr Majeika felt like. Although
he did feel sorry for Billy, the fact of the
matter was that Billy had *kidnapped* him.
But Mr Majeika had a plan.

'OK, Billy, I might be able to do the
spell for you, but all this bumping about
in the caravan has rattled my nerves. I
need to go somewhere quiet to collect
my thoughts or I won't be able to do any
magic.'

Billy looked unsure. But he did so

desperately need Mr Majeika's help. 'OK then,' he said, 'but don't take too long, the show will begin very soon.'

Mr Majeika walked away from the caravan and looked around. He needed a way to escape and get back to Class Three. Although he felt bad about lying to Billy, he had a strange feeling that Class Three were in trouble.

He couldn't escape through the entrance to the car park, because Hannibal the elephant had settled down right in the middle of it for a well-earned rest. There was a block of offices on the other side of the car park. Mr Majeika thought that if they had a back entrance on to the car park, there might be a front entrance on to the street which he could escape through. Failing that, he could always get to a top window, make himself invisible, and float home. He knew that he wasn't supposed to do magic in public, but this was an emergency. He quietly slipped through the door and into the offices.

Just as he got inside he heard voices, so he quickly hid behind the door and pressed himself up against the wall.

'I tried to get rid of them, Mr Midge, I really did, but even I am no match for an elephant that size.'

'Never mind,' said another voice, which Mr Majeika assumed was Mr Midge. 'They'll soon regret messing with me. Pathetic, tired, old has-beens. Their circus is already rubbish, but I'm going to make them a laughing stock! I'm going to make one of my famous "fly-on-the-wall" documentaries, and show the world how awful Mr Tottle's Circus really is.'

Mr Majeika didn't like what he was hearing. He was annoyed with Mr Tottle and Billy Balance for kidnapping him, but he knew that they were good people underneath, and they didn't deserve to have their lives ruined by a nasty little man like Midge.

'I'm going to call the programme *When Circuses Go Wrong*, and the highlight of the show is going to be when that ridiculous Billy Balance falls off the rope! He'll have to change his name – to Billy Wobble!'

That was it. Mr Majeika had grown quite fond of Billy and he would not have him made into a world-famous laughing stock. He crept back out into

the car park, found a quiet corner, and summoned up all his strength to do a rather large spell . . .

Back at St Barty's School, Class Three were running for their lives. They still hoped it was a dream, but Hamish Bigmore's lions were catching up with them, and there was nowhere to escape to. They were trapped inside an enormous circus tent – much bigger than Mr Tottle's Big Top – and all the doors to the outside world seemed to be blocked.

So Class Three went in the only direction where the lions couldn't follow them . . . up. They climbed the ladder and stood on the wooden perch leading to the slack rope. But when they looked down, the slack rope did not lead across the sawdust ring, but across a deep and dangerous river with crocodiles, and even a shark, splashing about in the water.

'Tee-hee!' said a voice that Class Three knew very well. 'I've got you all this time, you bunch of babies! That weaselly wizard Majeika won't help you now – he's run away with the circus, and you'll never see him again. I'm in charge now, and I'm going to let you fall into the river and be eaten up, mouthful by mouthful. Tee-hee! After all these years, I've won at last!'

The voice seemed to be coming from Mr Potter, or at least from one of the two Mr Potters in the tent, the one who was standing on the bank of the river. But the voice wasn't the voice of Mr Potter, it was the voice of Class Three's old enemy, Wilhelmina Worlock.

'So *that's* who it really was,' thought Jody. And as they all watched, Mr Potter turned into Wilhelmina.

'Go away, you stupid witch,' said Thomas. 'We're not frightened of you, and your river is fake – you don't have sharks in rivers, only in the sea.'

Wilhelmina laughed nastily. 'Maybe not, you silly little brat, but this one will munch you up just the same. Get ready to be eaten!' She waved her hands in the air, and the perch that they were all clinging on to started to shake. Hamish Bigmore began to complain.

'I'm your star pupil, Miss Worlock – you can't throw me to the crocodiles!'

But the perch just shook even more, and Class Three began to lose their balance. In a moment, they would be thrown into the river.

Then suddenly Mr Majeika appeared at the other end of the slack rope.

'Hello, everyone,' he said cheerily. 'I've come to fetch you all for a school trip to London!'

Miss Worlock squealed angrily. Mr Majeika's arrival had spoiled her spell, and the crocodile-infested river and the circus tent all vanished.

'You're coming too, Wilhelmina,' said Mr Majeika. 'We've got a lot of work to do and I'm going to need your help.'

'Me?' yelled Wilhelmina. 'But I'm your worst enemy.'

'You were,' said Mr Majeika, 'but I think I've found a worse enemy than even you.'

'A worse enemy than me?' said

Wilhelmina. 'Well, I can't allow that. Where is he? Just let me get at him!'

'Come along, everyone – there's no time to lose,' said Mr Majeika, and in the blink of an eye Class Three, Wilhelmina Worlock and Mr Majeika had all vanished, leaving a confused-looking Mr Potter scratching his head.

9. I'm a Celebrity

After the strange events of the day, Mr
Potter was looking forward to having a
quiet evening at home, watching
television. He turned on the television in
time for the teatime news. A few minutes
later, the newsreader began – but he was
suddenly interrupted by Hamish
Bigmore, who appeared in the studio,
pushing an enormous cannon on wheels.

'Go away!' hissed the newsreader.

'Go away, yourself,' answered Hamish
cheekily. 'You can't tell me where to go –
I'm a celebrity!'

Then an elephant came between the

camera and the newsreader, and Mr Potter's screen went grey.

'Anything on the news tonight?' called Mr Potter's wife from the kitchen.

'No, dear,' said Mr Potter, who for a moment thought he had seen Hamish Bigmore on television, but it couldn't be Hamish, because it was a Tuesday, and he knew that on Tuesdays Hamish Bigmore always went to tae kwon do classes. 'Nothing special,' said Mr Potter. 'Just the usual.'

At the television studio, everything was in total chaos. Hannibal the elephant was having the time of his life, wandering where he wanted, knocking things over, and picking up people who got in his way.

Class Three had arrived rather suddenly in the middle of the television studio, and to their delight found that they were still dressed in circus costumes.

'Oh thank goodness you're here,' said Mr Tottle, running up to Mr Majeika. 'We thought for a minute you had run away and that everything was going to be a disaster.'

'I would never do that,' said Mr Majeika (but he did look a little sheepish). 'Anyway, I've brought along some extra acts for your circus. I hope you don't mind, but I thought it could do with a few more young people in it.'

'Not at all,' said Mr Tottle. 'How delightful! The more the merrier!'

Mr Majeika looked over at Billy, who was standing in the wings. He could see that Billy was nervous, but so could Midge. Midge started to film Billy, pushing the camera right in his face and asking him, 'How do you feel, Billy? Are you worried that you might fall on live television?' This made Billy even more nervous, and his knees began to shake. Midge noticed this, and the camera zoomed in on Billy's knees.

'Please would you go away and leave Billy alone?' asked Mr Majeika.

'No I won't,' answered Midge. 'Don't pay any attention to me – treat me like a fly on the wall.'

'A fly on the wall you say?' came the voice of Wilhelmina Worlock. 'All right,' she said, 'if that's what you want to be.' And she closed her eyes and muttered a spell, and Midge turned into a fly, and buzzed around harmlessly with his tiny camera.

'That's the last time someone else tries to be Mr Majeika's worst enemy,' said Wilhelmina. 'I am his worst enemy in the world!'

And with that she vanished.

'I'm sure that won't be the last we see of her,' sighed Mr Majeika, 'but after all, I do suppose life at St Barty's would be rather dull without her wicked plans.'

When Midge was turned into a real fly on the wall, the television people did not know what to do or who was in charge. When Mr Tottle announced that there would be a circus performance in half an hour, and that it would be shown on television, they thought they might as well do as he said.

'What's more,' said Mr Tottle, 'Class Three will be taking part.' Everyone was very pleased about this, except Hamish Bigmore.

Jody was looking worried. She found Mr Majeika, and explained that, back at school, the spell he had sent them hadn't worked. 'So I'm worried about Billy,' she said. 'I don't think your spell is strong enough to stop him from falling.'

'Don't worry,' answered Mr Majeika. 'Everything will be fine. Trust me.'

'On air in five . . . four . . . three . . . two . . . one . . .' said the floor manager. And then they were on live television, being broadcast to the nation.

The show was a triumph. Jody did her balancing act on the horses, and this time she felt completely in control. Thomas and Pete were clowns and acrobats and really enjoyed themselves. Hannibal the elephant danced, and then Ivan the Terrible lifted him up with his bare hands.

The grand finale was, of course, Billy.

He had been watching everyone's acts from the wings, and he had seen people doing amazing things that he thought they couldn't possibly have done without Mr Majeika's magic. But he was still nervous, and the thought that he was on national television made it worse. He remembered the spell that Mr Majeika had taught him, and he sang it to himself under his breath as he climbed to the top of the slack rope:

'Those magnificent folk on the flying trapeze,
    They fly through the air with the greatest of ease.
Never ask how, and never ask why,
    But believe in yourself – you'll be able to fly.'

And then with all the confidence in the world he leapt out on to the rope and danced like he had never danced before. He pulled out his violin from inside his coat and began to play the song.

The rest of the circus, and the whole of
Class Three, joined in with Billy and
sang, 'Believe in yourself, you'll be able
to fly!' It was magnificent.

But just as they were all taking a final
bow, they heard an enormous BANG!
Hamish Bigmore crashed on to the
studio floor wearing a bright red helmet.
He had just shot himself out of the
cannon! The cameras all turned on to
Hamish and he stood up and shouted,

'Hello, world! This is Hamish Bigmore, human cannonball and exposer of tricks. I am here to tell you that Billy Balance is a fake and he would have fallen off the slack rope if it wasn't for Mr Majeika.'

Billy looked dejected. He had forgotten in the excitement of it all that he could only do his performance with Mr Majeika's help.

'Is that so?' said Mr Majeika. 'Well, let's see you try it then, Hamish.'

'Yeah I will,' said Hamish, and he climbed up to the perch at the end of the slack rope and chanted Mr Majeika's spell, word-for-word. But even holding on to the perch with one hand he wobbled so much that he had to go back.

'You must be blocking the magic!' said Hamish. 'I'll try it again, louder.' And he did, shouting as loud as he could (which in the case of Hamish Bigmore is very loud). He stepped on the rope and immediately

slid off, only just grabbing it with his
hands in time to haul himself back up.

'You see,' said Mr Majeika to Billy, 'that
rhyme I gave you wasn't really a spell
after all, just something to help you
believe in yourself. I always knew you
didn't really need my magic, if only you
could get back your own confidence.
You won't need me to help you with
your slack rope any more.'

'Oh, thank you so much, Mr Majeika!'
said Billy. 'But are you sure you don't
want to join the circus? Remember what
a magical life it can be!'

'No thank you, Billy,' said Mr Majeika. 'I have all the magic I need right here with Class Three.' And before Billy could say anything else he was gone, and so was the whole of Class Three.

Back home, Mr Potter was drinking the cup of hot water with which he always finished the evening. He thought that he had seen Mr Majeika and the whole of Class Three performing circus tricks on national television. But it couldn't have been. It just couldn't. Things like that never happened to children in his school. He switched off his television set.

'Was there anything good on television this evening, dear?' called Mr Potter's wife from the kitchen, where she was cleaning the oven.

'Not really,' said Mr Potter, giving an enormous yawn.